Ready for fun?

Enjoy these Ready-to-Read animal tales.

WISH AGAIN, BIG BEAR
By Richard J. Margolis/Illustrated by Robert Lopshire

Clever Fish bargains with Big Bear for his life. "Readable and entertaining—good fare for even the slowest." —*School Library Journal*

THE KOMODO DRAGON'S JEWELS
Written and illustrated by Diane Redfield Massie

A great, green lizard causes an uproar aboard a cruise ship in "a rollicking tale of mistaken identity." —*School Library Journal*

THE STORY SNAIL
Written and illustrated by Anne Rockwell

"[This] interlocking chain-of-events story about a boy's quest for the silver snail that has taught him 100 stories....possesses an artless simplicity." —*Booklist*

SOPHIE AND GUSSIE
By Marjorie Weinman Sharmat/Illustrated by Lillian Hoban

Four funny episodes in the best friendship of two squirrels. "The illustrations are plentiful, the heroines lovable, and the effect enjoyable." —*Library Journal*

THE TRIP
And Other Sophie and Gussie Stories
By Marjorie Weinman Sharmat/Illustrated by Lillian Hoban

More comical stories about the scatter-brained, charming squirrels first met in *Sophie and Gussie.*

MITCHELL IS MOVING
By Marjorie Weinman Sharmat/Illustrated by Jose Aruego and Ariane Dewey

Mitchell the dinosaur finds that a new home is not all good if his neighbor Margo isn't there in a warm and funny story about friendship.

HARRY AND SHELLBURT
By Dorothy O. Van Woerkom/Illustrated by Erick Ingraham

A.L.A. Notable 1977. A hilarious re-running of the famous race between the tortoise and the hare. "A memorable beginning reader." —*Booklist* (starred review)

DONKEY YSABEL
By Dorothy O. Van Woerkom/Illustrated by Normand Chartier

Donkey Ysabel's pride is hurt when Papa brings home a car—but she manages to get the best of the "new donkey."

LITTLE NEW KANGAROO
By Bernard Wiseman/Illustrated by Robert Lopshire

With Mother Kangaroo lending a helpful pouch, a young kangaroo picks up four friends on his first jaunt into the Australian countryside.

MACMILLAN PUBLISHING CO., INC.
866 Third Avenue, New York, N.Y. 10022

Marjorie Weinman Sharmat

The Trip

and Other Sophie and Gussie Stories

Pictures by Lillian Hoban

Ready-to-Read

Macmillan Publishing Co., Inc.
New York
Collier Macmillan Publishers
London

Remembering my aunts,
Frances Richardson Mack
Minnie Richardson Lelansky
Kate Richardson Emple

Macmillan Publishing Co., Inc., 866 Third Avenue, New York, N.Y. 10022
Collier Macmillan Canada, Ltd.
Printed in the United States of America

2 3 4 5 6 7 8 9 10

Library of Congress Cataloging in Publication Data
Sharmat, Marjorie Weinman. The trip, and other Sophie and Gussie stories.
(Ready-to-read) Summary: Two squirrel friends prepare for a trip,
clean house, listen to the rain, and care for a flower.
[1. Friendship—Fiction. 2. Squirrels—Fiction. 3. Short stories]
I. Hoban, Lillian. II. Title.
PZ7.S5299Tr   [E]   76–10168   ISBN 0-02-782300-8

Contents

The Trip

Gussie was putting some clothes
into a suitcase.
"I am going on a trip,"
she said to Sophie.
"Where are you going?" asked Sophie.
"I don't know yet," said Gussie.

"It will be someplace where
I can see old things and new things
and do exciting things."
"I will miss you," said Sophie.
"I will send you a postcard,"
said Gussie.
"May I help you pack?" asked Sophie.
"Yes," said Gussie. "Would you please
bring me my yellow hat?

It is in my closet."

Sophie went to the closet.

"I don't see a yellow hat,"

she said.

"I will look," said Gussie.

Gussie went to the closet.

She looked up and down.

"I don't see my yellow hat either,"

she said. "Maybe it is in the attic."

Sophie and Gussie went to the attic.
"This is where I keep the things
I have had for a long time,"
said Gussie.
"You have a lot of cobwebs and dust,"
said Sophie.
"Yes, I have had them
for a long time," said Gussie.
Sophie and Gussie looked for
the yellow hat.
They looked at everything in the attic.
There was no yellow hat.
"Maybe you don't have a yellow hat,"
said Sophie.

"Maybe I don't," said Gussie.

She brushed the cobwebs and dust
out of her clothes.

Sophie and Gussie went downstairs.
Gussie lay down on her couch.
"I am tired from looking
   at all those things," she said.
"But I need a yellow hat
   to go with my yellow dress."

"Well then, let's go to the store
and buy a yellow hat," said Sophie.
"That's a good idea," said Gussie.
They got ready and went to town.

Gussie tried on many yellow hats.
At last she found one
that looked just right. Then she said,
"While I am in the store,
I think I will buy some other things
for my trip."
Gussie bought and bought and bought.
At last she had many packages.
"I will help you carry them
home," said Sophie.
When they got to Gussie's house,
Gussie opened her packages.

"There is one package missing,"
she said.

"Which one?" asked Sophie.

"The one that had my yellow hat
in it," said Gussie. And she
lay down on her couch.

"You must get up," said Sophie.

"We must look for your hat."

They walked back
the way they had come.
"Look, there is your hat box,"
said Sophie.
"You are a good finder
and a good friend," said Gussie,
picking up the box.
Sophie and Gussie went back
to Gussie's house.

"I can hardly wait to see
how this hat will look
with my yellow dress," said Gussie.
"Neither can I," said Sophie.
"I will get your dress for you."
Sophie went to the closet.
"I don't see a yellow dress," she said.
"I will look," said Gussie.

Gussie went to the closet.

"I don't see a yellow dress either,"
   she said. Then she said to Sophie,
"I know why we cannot find
   my yellow dress."

"Why?" asked Sophie.

"Because I do not have
   a yellow dress," said Gussie.

"Last summer I threw my
yellow dress away."
Gussie got her suitcase.
She started to unpack.
"Why are you unpacking?"
asked Sophie.

"Because I don't need this trip,"
said Gussie.
"I saw old things in my attic
and new things in the store,
and I lost and found my hat.
I have had enough old and new
and exciting things to last me
for a long, long time."

"I am glad I won't have to miss you," said Sophie. And she put Gussie's suitcase back in the closet.

The Problem

One morning Gussie called Sophie.

"What are you doing today?" she asked.

"Working hard," said Sophie.

"Working hard?" said Gussie.

"Yes, I am washing and waxing
and dusting," said Sophie.

"I worked hard yesterday,"
said Gussie.

"Today is my sitting day.

Do you mind if I come over and sit?"

"Come," said Sophie.

Gussie went to Sophie's house.

Sophie was scrubbing the floor.

"You <u>are</u> working hard today,"
said Gussie.

"Yes," said Sophie. And she
squeezed the water from her rag.

"Do you mind if I help myself
to a cup of tea?" asked Gussie.

"Help yourself," said Sophie.

Gussie got a cup of tea.
"Would you like some?"
she asked Sophie.
"No, I can't sip and work,"
said Sophie.

"I will hold the cup
to your lips," said Gussie.
"That will be nice," said Sophie.
Gussie held and Sophie sipped.

Then Gussie sat down.

She took a sip.

"How nice it is to sit," she said.

"Yes, I remember," said Sophie.

"I sat the day before yesterday."

"The day before yesterday?"
said Gussie. "What have you
been doing since then?"

"Working hard," said Sophie.

And she squeezed out her rag again.

"Why are you working so hard?"
asked Gussie.

"Because I want my house
to be nice," said Sophie.

"Your house is always nice,"
said Gussie.

"But I want it to be
   as nice as it can be," said Sophie.
"Do you mind if I have
   another cup of tea?" asked Gussie.

"Help yourself," said Sophie.

Gussie filled her cup.

She sat down and sipped her tea.

Then she said, "I have a problem."

"What is it?" asked Sophie.

"I cannot sit here
and watch you work," said Gussie.
"What are you going to do
about it?" asked Sophie.
"I am going home," said Gussie.
"Oh," said Sophie.
Gussie went home.
Sophie rinsed her rag
and scrubbed another floor.
There was a knock on the door.
Sophie answered it.
It was Gussie.
"I still have a problem," she said.
"What is it?" asked Sophie.

"I cannot sit at home and
   think about your working so hard."
"Think about something else,"
   said Sophie.
"I can't," said Gussie.
"When I look at a floor,
   I think of you scrubbing.

When I look at a chair,

I think of you dusting.

When I look at a sink,

I think of you washing."

"You have a problem," said Sophie.

"Come in."

Gussie walked in.

"There is only one thing

to do," she said.

"I know it," said Sophie.

She gave Gussie her apron.

She gave Gussie her rag.

She gave Gussie her pail.

"There is an answer

to every problem," said Sophie.

And she sat down.

Gussie started to scrub.

"You are right," she said.

"My problem has gone away."

"I know it," said Sophie.

"Now I have it. I cannot sit here and watch you work."

Gussie stood up.

"Your house is as nice

as it can be," she said.

"Do you really think so?" said Sophie.

"I really think so," said Gussie.

"Want to pick some violets?"

asked Sophie.

"I really think so," said Gussie.

And they went out into the forest.

The Ceiling

One evening, rain was falling hard.
Gussie called Sophie.
"There is a leak in my ceiling,"
she said. "Can you come over?"
"I will be right over," said Sophie.
Sophie got an umbrella
and she went to Gussie's house.

"I have come to help," she said.

"I don't need help," said Gussie.

"I need company."

Gussie sat down.

Sophie sat down.

"I have never sat and watched
a leak before," said Sophie.

"Neither have I," said Gussie.

"Why do we have to
watch it?" asked Sophie.
"Because you never know
what a leak will do," said Gussie.
"Oh," said Sophie.
"Tomorrow someone is coming
to fix it," said Gussie.
"That is good," said Sophie.

"Would you like a chocolate?"
asked Gussie.

"I would love a chocolate," said Sophie.

"These are delicious," said Gussie.

"Yes, they are," said Sophie.

"Would you like to play checkers?"
asked Gussie.

"When it is your turn,
I can watch the leak.
When it is my turn,
you can watch the leak."

"I would love to play checkers,"
said Sophie.

"Will you be red or black?" asked Gussie.

"Which is better?" asked Sophie.

"They are both the same," said Gussie.

"No, they aren't.

One is red and one is black.

43

"I will take half and half," said Sophie.

"You can't," said Gussie.

"You have to take all red or all black."

"I can't decide," said Sophie.

"Listen. I think the leak
   is doing something new."

"What's that?" asked Gussie.

"When I came, it was leaking
'drip, drip, drip,'" said Sophie.
"Now it is leaking 'drip, pause...
drip, pause...drip, pause.'"
"You're right," said Gussie.
"You have sharp eyes."
"Ears," said Sophie.

"Isn't it interesting to watch
   a leak?" said Gussie.
"Very interesting," said Sophie.
"May I have another chocolate?"
"Of course," said Gussie.
   And she gave Sophie a chocolate.

"Would you like to sing a song
   while we watch?" asked Gussie.
"Why not?" said Sophie.
"What should we sing?"
"Let's sing 'Nuts in May,'" said Gussie.
And they sang, "Here we go gathering
nuts in May, nuts in May, nuts in May,
on a bright and sunny morning."

"That was nice," said Gussie
when they finished.
Sophie said, "Listen, there is a new
sound. Now the leak is going
'drip, pause…drip, pause…pause.'"
"You are a terrific listener," said Gussie.
"I don't hear the rain any more,"
said Sophie.
"And now the leak has stopped.
There is only 'pause…pause…pause.'"
"You are right," said Gussie.
"There is no more leak."

"There is nothing more
   for us to watch," said Sophie.
"So I will go home."
"Thank you for coming," said Gussie.
"You're welcome," said Sophie.

Sophie got her umbrella
and walked home.
"What a silly way
to spend an evening," she said.

The Flower

Sophie and Gussie were
walking in the forest.

"Oh," said Sophie.

"Look at that beautiful flower."

"It is beautiful," said Gussie.

"It's the most beautiful flower
I have ever seen."

"I have a vase that would be
just right for that flower,"
said Sophie.

"So have I," said Gussie.

"Well then, you take the flower,"
  said Sophie.
"No," said Gussie. "You saw it first.
  It's your flower."
"No, you may have it," said Sophie.
"No, you may have it," said Gussie.
"Let's not decide today," said Sophie.
"All right," said Gussie.
  The next day Sophie got up early.
  She took a watering can.
  She went to the forest
  and found the flower.
"A beautiful flower like you
  should have a long and happy life,"
  she said. "Drink."

And she watered the flower.
Along came Gussie
with a watering can.
"I just watered the flower,"
said Sophie.
"A lovely flower needs
a lot of water," said Gussie.

And she, too, watered the flower.

That afternoon Gussie packed
a picnic lunch.

She took her lunch basket
and walked to the flower.

Sophie was there.

"Come keep us company," said Sophie.

"All right," said Gussie.

And she sat down.

"You are making a shadow
over the flower," said Sophie.

"If the flower doesn't get sun
it will die."

"You are making a shadow, too,"

said Gussie. "If you move,

I will move."

"I will sit here awhile

and think about it," said Sophie.

"So will I," said Gussie.

And they did.

The next day Gussie took her vase
off a shelf and took it to the flower.
She put it over the flower.
Along came Sophie.
"What are you doing?" asked Sophie.
"I am seeing how the flower would
look in my vase," said Gussie.

"Upside down?" said Sophie.

"Yes," said Gussie.

"If it looks good upside down,
it will certainly look good
right side up."

"I brought my vase, too," said Sophie.

"Let me try it on the flower."
Gussie lifted her vase off.
Sophie put her vase over the flower.

"My vase looks fine over the flower,"
said Sophie.

"Yes, it does," said Gussie.

"Your vase looks fine
and my vase looks fine."

"But," said Sophie.

"But what?" said Gussie.

"The flower looks wilted," said Sophie.

"We made it wilt.
We gave it too much water.
We shaded it from the sun.
We squeezed it into our vases.
Now we have a wilted flower."

"Oh, dear," said Gussie.

"What do we do now?"

"We leave it alone," said Sophie.
"We leave it to grow as it was growing
before it met us. Let's go home."

A few days later
Gussie said to Sophie,
"Do you think we should go
and take a peek at our flower?"
"Yes," said Sophie.
They went to the forest.

"I think our flower looks
  better," said Gussie.
"Yes, it does," said Sophie.
"Let's come back again tomorrow
  and see how it is," said Gussie.
"That's a good idea," said Sophie,
  and they started for home.

"Sometimes it is nicer
to have something together
than separately," said Sophie.
"I think so, too," said Gussie.